D1093231

REGULAR SHOW™
HYDRATION

REGULAR SHOW: HYDRATION, September 2014. Published by KaBOOM!, a division of Boom Entertainment, Inc. REGULAR SHOW, CARTO

For information regarding the CPSIA on this printed material, call: (203) 595-3636 and provide reference #RICH – 566917. A catalog record of book is available from OCLC and from the KaBOOM! website, www.kaboom-studios.com, on the Librarians Page.

BOOM! Studios, 5670 Wilshire Boulevard, Suite 450, Los Angeles, CA 90036-5679. Printed in USA. First Printing.

ISBN: 978-1-60886-339-6, eISBN: 978-1-61398-193-1

REGULAR SHOW™

HYDRATION

CREATED BY **JG QUINTEL**

WRITTEN BY
RACHEL CONNOR

ILLUSTRATED BY
TESSA STONE

COLORS BY
RED STRESING
WITH WHITNEY COGAR

LETTERS BY
COREY BREEN

COVER BY
ALLISON STREJLAU

DESIGNER
KARA LEOPARD

ASSISTANT EDITOR
WHITNEY LEOPARD

EDITOR
SHANNON WATTERS

WITH THANKS TO ROBERT LUCKETT AND A VERY SPECIAL THANKS TO MARISA MARIONAKIS, RICK BLANCO, JEFF PARKER, LAURIE HALAL-ONO, NICOLE RIVERA, CONRAD ONTGOMERY, MEGHAN BRADLEY, CURTIS LELASH AND THE WONDERFUL FOLKS AT CARTOON NETWORK.

UGH. THIS HEATWAVE KIBOSHES ALL OUR OUTDOOR SUMMER FUN DAY-OFF PLANS.

LAME! IF WE'RE STAYING IN I NEED SOMETHING TO TAKE MY MIND OFF THE HEAT, BRO! I'M GETTING THE SUN-SCRITCHIES! ARGH!
BEEN SAVING A SPECIAL SOMETHING FOR JUST THIS SORT OF DAY...
KER-GAME!
CUZZO'S
YAY-YEAHHHH!

ICE CUZZO'S
HMM-HMM.

SCORE
0020
LEVEL ONE:
CLIMB! CLIMB!
x03

SCORE 024127
x03
YOU DO REALIZE YOU'RE THE STRIPY SNOW CUZZO AND NOT MY CHECKER-BRO PLAYER, RIGHT?
SHUT UP! I'M FOCUSING ON ENJOYING THE HI-DEF ICY ATMOSPHERE!

JUST FOLLOW MY LEAD, DUDE. I WANT TO SEE ALL THE BOARDS OF THIS GAME.
COOL. COOL.

THOSE THINGS ARE DEATH, DUDE! WHAT DID I JUST TELL YOU?
THEY LOOK LIKE REFRESHING ICE-POPS THOUGH!
SIGH
STRATEGY CHANGE: JUST PRESS ATTACK WHEN I SAY.
200
300
HAND FAILURE!

FAILING AT VIDEOGAMES HAS NEVER FELT SO GOOOOD...
THIS WAS A RARE CART, DUDE. YOU GONNA BRING YOUR A-GAME OR WHAT?
OKAY. OKAY. BEATING MODE: ACTIVATED! GEEZ.

LEVEL FINAL

CLIMB!
CLIMB!
SNAP!
DEATH

WHY IS THERE ALWAYS A LAVA LEVEL? WHY?!

GAME OVER

DO YOU THINK SKIPS HAS ICE BREATH POWERS LIKE THAT BOSS MONSTER?
NO DUDE, DON'T THINK SO. QUIT YOUR GROSS SCRATCHING TOO, PLEASE.
MY AWESOME BODY TYPE DOESN'T *LIKE* HEATWAVES! I DEMAND YOU TO FAN ME IMMEDIATELY!

WHAT?! NO, FAN YOURSELF!

YOU'RE REAL GOOD AT FANNING THOUGH, BRAH!
THEN I'LL JUST GET TOO HOT FROM FANNING YOU! FIND YOUR OWN WAY TO KEEP COOL.

...COOLNESS...

THE SOURCE OF ALL COOLNESS! YOU WON'T LET ME DOWN!
DUDE! WHAT ARE YOU DOING?!
MAKING SPACE!
SO SORRY MORDECAI. LOOKS LIKE THERE'S ONLY ENOUGH SPACE FOR ME. FIND YOUR OWN WAY TO KEEP COOL!
SLAM

UGH, THE LIGHT'S GONE OUT.
YES, THAT'S HOW IT WORKS, DINGUS.
THAT'S FINE. FINE. NOT CREEPY IN HERE. NOPE. JUST REFRESHING.
JUST GOT TO THINK SUPER-CHILL THOUGHTS. ENTER TOTAL CHILL-BRO MODE.
OMMMMMMMM...
ONE HOUR LATER...
BRO, ARE YOU ALRIGHT IN THERE?
OMMMMMMMMMMMMMM

WHAT.
'TIS A HOT-BLOODED APOCALYPSE!
I SEEK ONLY ICINESS IN PEACE!

AHHH!
DESTROY THE RED BEAST OF RAGNAROK!
BOMBS AWAY!
COLA
AGH! CEASE! OW!
RAAAAAAAAHHHHHHHH!
BEST BY: 2/3/14
COLA

O-O-OOPS.

I WAS EXPERIENCING ICY BRAIN BAD DREAMS. HOW DID YOU THAW ME OUT THAT QUICK?
THAT'S HOW HOT IT IS OUT HERE, YOU CHILD. NOW WE WON'T BE HAVING COLD SODAS ANYTIME SOON EITHER, THANKS TO YOU.
OKAY, OKAY, SORRY! GEEZ, *MOM.*
WHATEVER. WHILE YOU WERE ON YOUR ICEBOX ADVENTURE, I READ THAT HOT DRINKS ARE BEST FOR COOLING DOWN IN SUMMER.
WHAT, LIKE COFFEE
MORDECAI: N
DUDE. YOU'R
HYPER ENOUG
TODAY.
LET'S MAKE HOT-JUICE INSTEAD.
BEST BY: 3/4
MADE FROM 1.25764% JUICE
OJ
BEST BY 3/4
MADE FROM 1.25764% JUICE
OJ

A COUPLE OF MINUTES LATER...
I STILL DON'T SEE HOW THIS'LL WORK.
DON'T FIGHT SCIENCE, DUDE.

SSSSIP
AHHH.

ITS NOT WORKINGGGG!
GIVE IT A CHANCE!

AND NOW, MORE WORLDS' MOST WILD WHALES!
WHAAARGGGH!
IT'S NOT WORKING, MORDECAI. I FEEL LIKE I'M ABOUT TO EXPLODE...
GEEZ! HOW MUCH DID YOU DRINK?!
NOT ENOUGH, CLEARLY! I'M SWEATIER THAN *EVER!* THE MAIN INGREDIENT OF HOT-JUICE IS CLEARLY *HOT LIES!*

THAT'S HOW IT WORKS! YOUR BODY. SWEATING IS ITS WAY OF LOWERING YOUR TEMPERATURE. SO A HOT DRINK WILL...

MAKE ME SWEAT MORE?! NO. THE SWEATING IS WHAT *I DIDN'T WANT!*

OH!

YOUR GROSS SLOSHING SOUNDS JUST REMINDED ME OF SOMETHING I SAW IN POPS' CLOSET ONCE!
WHATEVER, YOUR *FACE* IS MAKING SLOSHING SOUNDS...

MINUTES LATER...
BEHOLD!

EEMED
REASURED ODDITY
and PROPERTY OF
POPS
POPS' POOL!
YES, DUDE! YES!
ESTEEME
TREASURED ODDI
and PROPERTY OF
POPS
SQUEEZE!
SQUOOOOH!
ESTEEMED
TREASURED ODDITY
POPS
I SAW POPS BLOW THIS THING UP OVER AN ENTIRE DAY AND IT NEARLY DID HIM IN. THAT'S WHY IT'S NEVER BEEN DEFLATED...

ESTEEMED TREASURED ODDITY POPS
OHHHHHHHHHHHHH!!
THIS IS OPERATION: BEST PLAN EVER! ONCE THE POOL'S FILLED UP...
...WE CAN KICK BACK, WATCH SOME WRASSLIN' AND LIFE IS TOTALLY SWEET AGAIN!

C
FILLED!

AS WAY OF APOLOGY FOR THE LAVA POOL, FIRST DIBS IS YOURS, RIGBONE.

SPLASH

AHHHHHHHHHHHHHH.

PREPARE YOURSELF! FOR...
NO, NOT THAT! NOT A GOOD IDEA!
...THE MORDO-BOMB OF DOOM!

SPLORT!
DUDE! ARE YOU AND YOUR SCHNOZZ FOR REAL?!
BA-BURST!

SAVE THE VIDEOGAMES! ALL ELSE IS LOST!
SORRY. MY BAD.

WELL, THIS IS EASILY SOLVED. HANG TIGHT...
OH NO... CLOSE THE WINDOW, DUDE!
PWOOF!

AN HOUR LATER...
THIS SAUNA WAS RELAXING AT FIRST, BUT NOW... ≷COUGH≶
I'M DYING. THIS IS WHAT DYING FEELS LIKE. HAS THE SUN GONE DOWN YET?
LOOKS LIKE IT. WE CAN'T SLEEP IN THIS STEAM-PIT, BRO. LET'S EVACUATE.
ONE TICK. MAYBE BENSON WILL BE PLEASED WE STEAM-CLEANED THE PLACE?
DOUBT IT, DUDE. HURRY UP, THE VAPORS ARE GETTING TO ME.

SO WE'RE SLEEPING ALL FRESHCO TONIGHT?
AL FRESCO. SLEEPING UNDER THE STARS CAN BE CHILLAXING, DUDE.
I'LL BE CHILLAXED AS LONG AS YOU AND YOUR UNIQUELY POINTY FACE STOP RUINING MY LIFE. IS IT GOING TO BE COOLER TOMORROW?
THE WEATHER CHANNEL WAS SAYING IT'LL BE A DEGREE COOLER, SO NOT MUCH.

IT FEELS EVEN HOTTER NOW THOUGH! AND THE SUN'S NOT EVEN OUT...

MAYBE BECAUSE THE MOON WAS THE SECRET HEAT-MAKER ALL ALONG! DARN MOON! MORDECAI? BRAH?
ZZZ

A-A SHOOTING STAR...A WISH...
BRING BACK... THE COOLNESS... UNTO MEEEE--

ZZZ

KRAKOOM

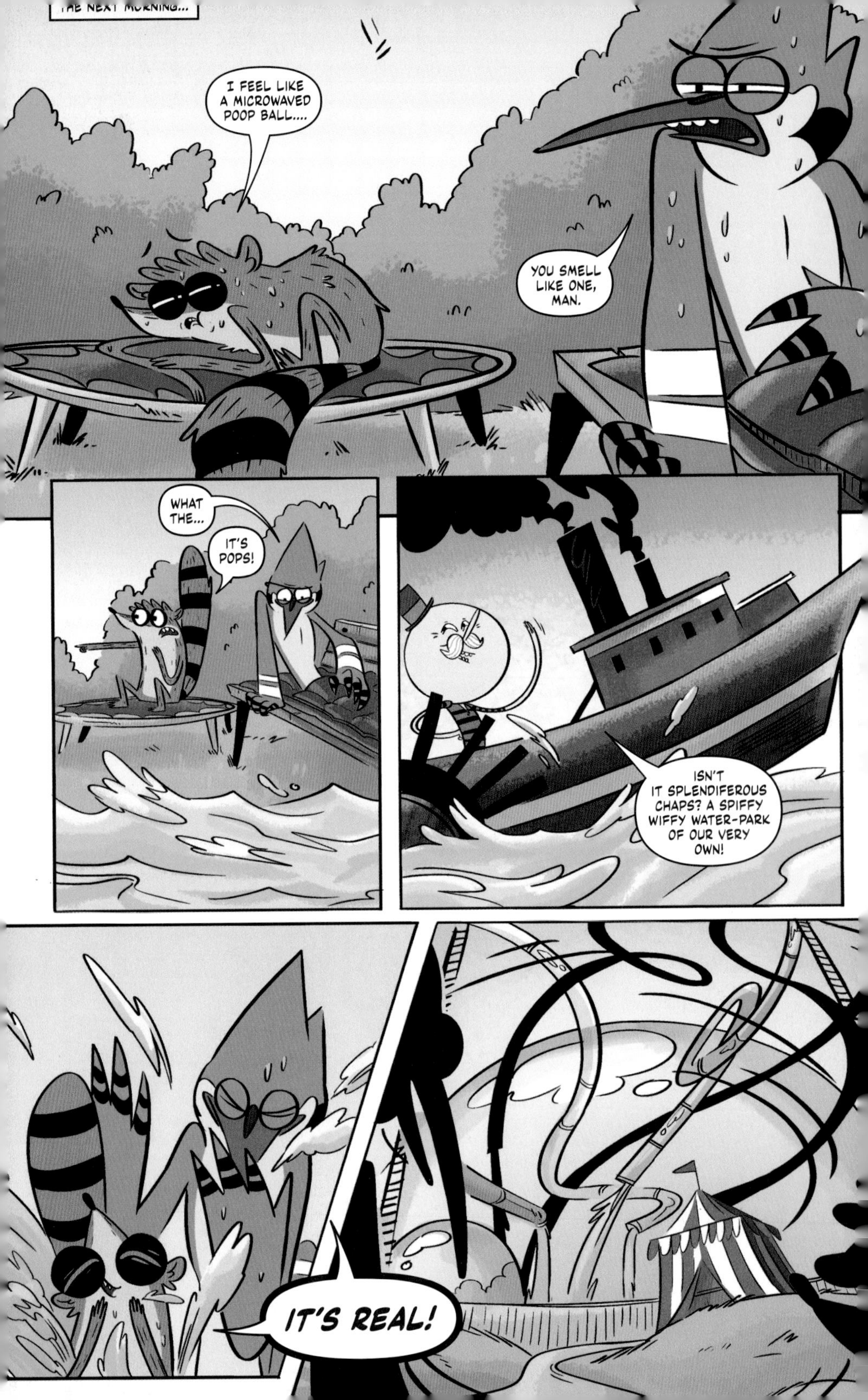
THE NEXT MORNING...
I FEEL LIKE A MICROWAVED POOP BALL....
YOU SMELL LIKE ONE, MAN.
WHAT THE...
IT'S POPS!
ISN'T IT SPLENDIFEROUS CHAPS? A SPIFFY WIFFY WATER-PARK OF OUR VERY OWN!
IT'S REAL!

WOAH!
WOAH!

MY WISH CAME TRUE! I HAVE WISH POWERS NOW, MORDECAI!
ADMISSION
EITHER THAT OR BENSON DOES, DUDE.
WHAT'S WRONG WITH HIS FACE?
I THINK HE'S... SMILING.
BOYS! IT'S A CHRISTMAS IN JULY MIRACLE! PLENTY OF WORK FOR YOU TWO TO BE GETTING ON WITH TOO.
AWWWW, MAN.
HEY GUYS!
WEEE HEE HEE--!

OHHHH IT'S SIMPLY THE MOST FUN IN THE ENTIRE WORLD!
THERE'S NO WAY I'M WORKING BEFORE TRYING OUT THESE SUPER-SWEET SLIDES FIRST!
SO HOW DID THIS GET HERE ANYHOO?
NO IDEA, IT WAS HERE FIRST THING THIS MORNING...
ALSO SKIPS, DO YOU HAVE ICY BREATH POWERS?
I CAN NEITHER CONFIRM NOR DENY.

WE SHOULD GET MUSCLE MAN OUT HERE, THIS SEEMS LIKE HIS JAM!
EHEHEHEH. BAD IDEA, DUDE. HE'S KINDA ALLERGIC TO WATERSLIDES NOW.
AND HOT DOG EATING CONTESTS. FOR THE FOREVERS.
UH-UH! NO WAY AM I HAVING MUSCLE MAN BREAK THESE SLIDES OR SPOILING THE MOOD JUST BECAUSE HE DIED ONCE ON HIS OWN DEATH-TRAP!
THOMAS! NEW JOB FOR YOU. GO TO MUSCLE MAN'S TRAILER AND KEEP HIM BUSY AND AWAY FROM HERE ALL DAY!
AWWWW MAN.

THIS MEANS MORE JOBS FOR YOU TWO. KEEP A GOOD LOOK OUT AND MAKE SURE NOBODY GETS INTO TROUBLE. SAFETY IS MY MAIN CONCERN!
ARE YOU SERIOUS? WORK IN TH HEAT?!
WE WANT IN!
NEW POLICY! ENTRANTS AFTER 9AM PAY $5 MORE!
SAFETY IS HIS MAIN CONCERN, HUH?

SO HOW ARE THE SLIDES, HUH? HUH?
BRO, YOU MUST BE HATING THIS HEATWAVE TOO. DO THE SLIDES COOL YOUR HEAT SCRATCHIES?
I AIN'T TRIED 'EM YET. THIS WHOLE PARK IS GIVING ME THE *EVIL KNIEVELS...*
OOOOHHHH! SKIPS IS SCARED OF WATERSLIDES! MIGHT MESS UP HIS MULLET! H 2 OOOOHHHH!
I AIN'T SCARED!

PROOOOVE IT.
I WILL.
I'M GOING TO INVESTIGATE. DON'T DO ANYTHING STUPID WHILE I'M GONE.
WE WON'T!
NOW FEELS LIKE A FAR MOR APPROPRIATE TIM TO BREAK OUT..
YESSSS!
...THE MORDO-BOMB...
...OF LESSER-DOOM!
YAY-YEAH!
KER-SPLOOSH!

MAAAARCCCOOOO--!
POLO?
POLO?
NO! MY LITTLE BOY MARCO WENT UP TO THE TOP SLIDE AND NOW I CAN'T FIND HIM!
NOT TO WORRY MA'AM. I WAS JUST ABOUT TO ENJ-- INVESTIGATE THE TOP SLIDE MYSELF.
MM-MM. I'LL KEEP WATCH DOWN HERE.

WOOSSH
OH MAN...
STILL SO FULL... OF HOT-JUICE...
HMM. NO SIGN OF THE KID OR SKIPS. I GUESS HE REALLY IS SCARED OF WATER SLIDES.
PEAK ACHIEVED
QUICKEST WAY DOWN IS THE FUN WAY ROUND! ALLEY OOP!

AAAAAAAA

AAAAAAAAAAA

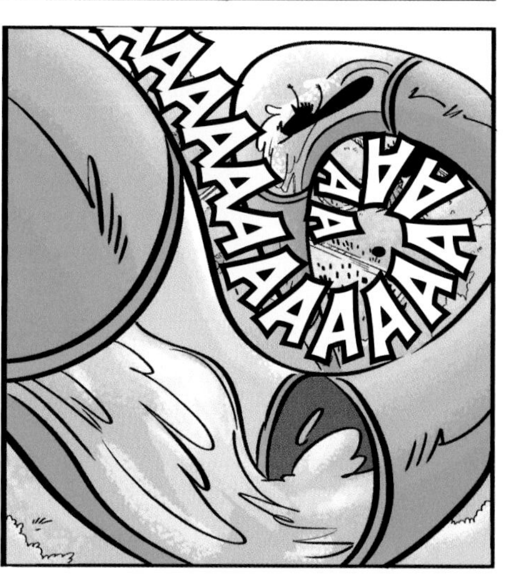
AAAAAAAAAAAAAA

GURGLE

BOOURRP!

EWWWWW!
SO GROSS. THE GROSSEST.
POOR EXIT, DUDE.

WASN'T ME. WHATEVER. I CAN'T EXPRESS MYSELF WITH ALL THIS HOT JUICE IN MY BELLY.

ANY SIGN OF MARCO?
...POLO...
NOPE, NO SIGN OF SKIPS EITHER. HE TOTALLY WUSSED OUT ON DOING THE SLIDE!

JACUZZI NEXT!
THAT DOESN'T SEEM LIKE SKIPS...

NO SIGN OF HIM HERE, MAYBE WE SHOULD CHECK THE BALL PIT INSTEAD...
SUUUREEE, JUST AFTER ONE MINUTE OF PURE REEEELAXATION...
OH NO DUDE, IT'S BENSON!
OHMAIGAWD!

ER...
THIS IS A JACUZZI, BRO. NOT A JACU-PEE!

DUDE...
EWWWWWWW!
...

IT'S NOT MY FAULT. MORDECAI FORCED ME TO DRINK A TON OF HOT-JUICE!
THE WORST PEE STINK EVER. THE WORST.
SMELLS LIKE BURNING TIRES!
OF COURSE YOU'D FIND A WAY TO RUIN THIS! OF COURSE.
H-HELP MORDO...

DUDE... DUDE...THIS IS THE MOST HEINOUS... GROSSEST...
IF YOU DON'T FIND A WAY TO SMOOTH THIS ALL OVER, YOU'RE BOTH FIRED!
PLEASE HELP, MORDECAI! I COULDN'T HELP IT. T-THE BUBBLES AND THE RELAXATION AND...
NO WAY AM I HELPING TO CLEAN UP THIS GRODY MESS, YOU'RE ON YOUR OWN!

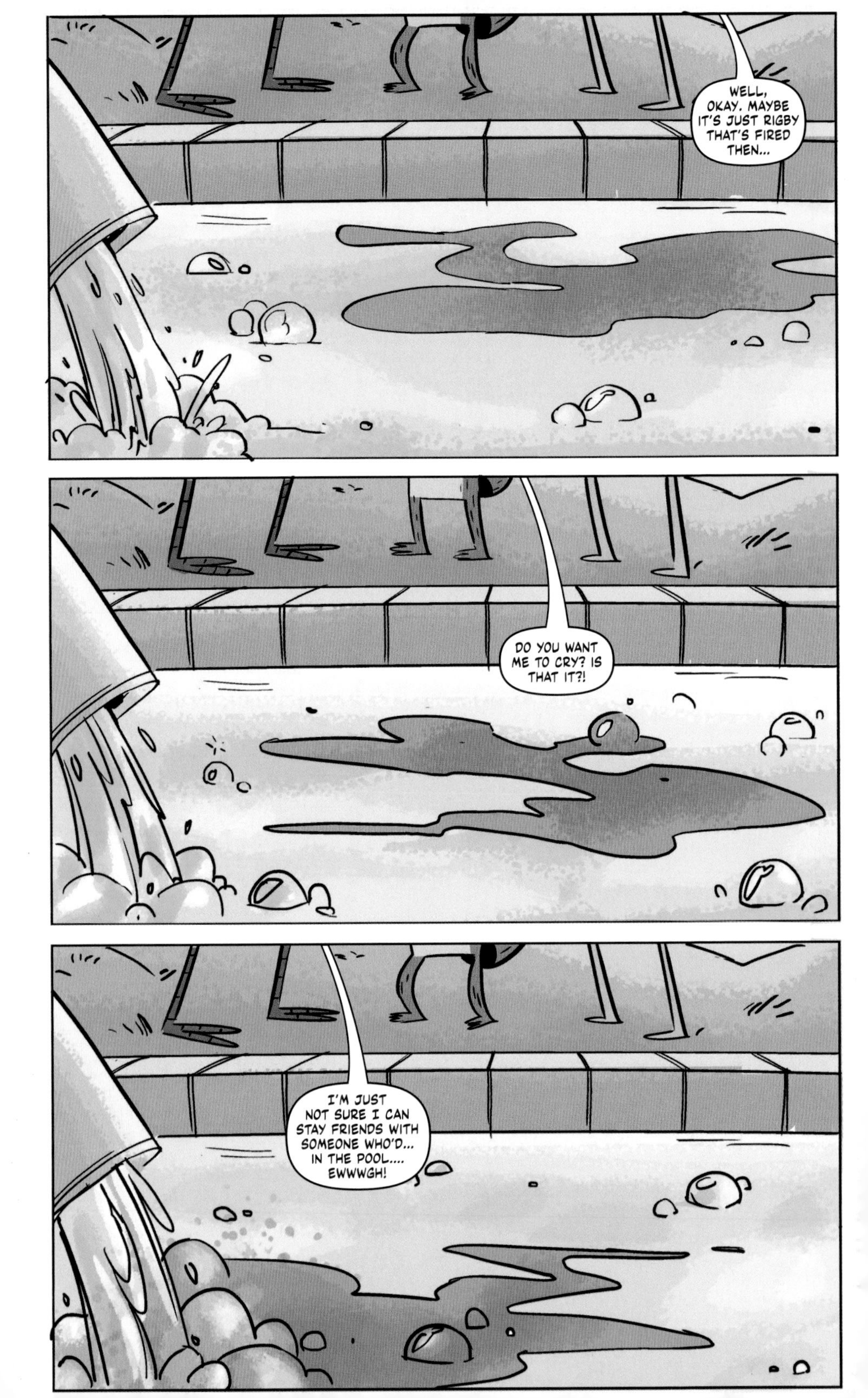
WELL, OKAY. MAYBE IT'S JUST RIGBY THAT'S FIRED THEN...
DO YOU WANT ME TO CRY? IS THAT IT?!
I'M JUST NOT SURE I CAN STAY FRIENDS WITH SOMEONE WHO'D... IN THE POOL.... EWWWGH!

BUBBLE!
BUBBLE!

COUGH

PSSS

SSS!

OH CRIPES!
GULP!

MY CHRISTMAS IN JULY MIRACLE... THIS IS ALL YOUR FAULT!
YEAH, SURE. IT'S ALL MY FAULT, WE DISCOVERED THIS GIANT SNAKE MONSTER BECAUSE OF MY BRAVE AND VERY PUBLIC SACRIFICE.
TOTALLY NOT BUYING IT DUDE. SUPER-GROSS AND UNFORGIVEABLE!
MAAAARCCCOOOO--!
...POLO...
...POLO...
RATTLE RATTLE!

AAAAAAAAAA!
NOOOOOOOOOO--
WHEEEEEEEEE--
NOOOO! BAD SNAKEY WAKEY!
goph

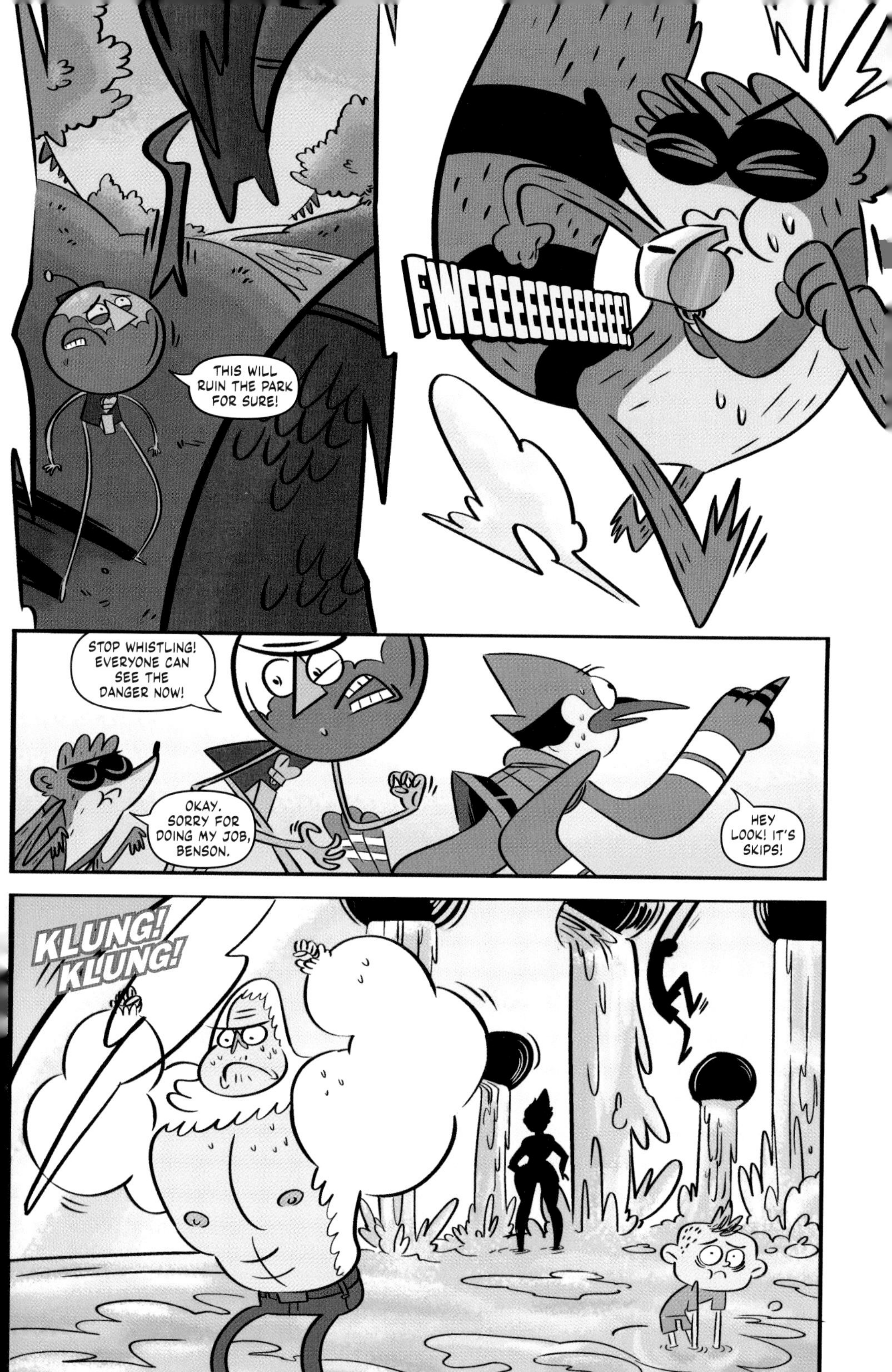
THIS WILL RUIN THE PARK FOR SURE!
FWEEEEEEEEEEEEE!
STOP WHISTLING! EVERYONE CAN SEE THE DANGER NOW!
OKAY. SORRY FOR DOING MY JOB, BENSON.
HEY LOOK! IT'S SKIPS!
KLUNG! KLUNG!

FEELIN' PRETTY GUILTY ABOUT DARING SKIPS ONTO THE SLIDES RIGHT ABOUT NOW.
YUUUUUUP.
IT LOOKS LIKE HE'S TRYING TO TELL US SOMETHING...

NOOOO LICKS FOR SNAKEY LIPS!
POPS! QUICK, INTO THESE CONVENIENT CHANGING ROOMS!
HSSS?

M-MAYBE WE'LL BE SAFE IN HERE FOR A MOMENT?

THLWIP
SAFETY DENIED!

AN ANIMATRONIC WATER-PARK? THAT IS TOOOOTES GENIUS.
SWIMMING AND A SHOW! SIMPLY MAAAARVELOUS.
I'VE BEEN WAITING SINCE 1999 FOR SOMETHING THIS X-TREME, BRAH!
BEEFY-BUNGA!

WE NEED TO TAKE THIS THING DOWN!
MM-MM!
YOU TAKE THE HIGH ROAD RIGBY! I'LL GET ITS ATTENTION DOWN HERE...

GOTCHA!

YO SNAKE! YO MOMMA WAS A LEAKY GARDEN HOSE!

FWEEEEEEEE
TWO FER ONE! YAY-YEAAAAHHHH!

WELL... MAYBE NOBODY NEEDS TO BE FIRED TODAY AFTER ALL, NOW...
HEY LOOK! SKIPS IS CHEERING FOR US! DON'T WORRY SKIPS, WE GOT THIS.
KLUNG! KLUNG!
I DUNNO, DUDE. HE SEEMS TICKED. I HOPE THIS ISN'T AN ANIMAL CRUELTY HANG UP. SNAKY CHOPS WAS OUT TO EAT *US*.

KER-SPLOOSH!
RRRRUMBLE
UM, GENTLEMENS, I HATE TO INTERRUPT YOUR MERRYMAKING BUT...

OH. SKIPS WAS TRYING TO TELL US IT'S A HYDRA.

WELP, WE GAVE IT OUR BEST SHOT. TIME TO CLOCK OUT FOR THE DAY. YOU WIT ME OL' BIRD BUDDY?

JUST PREPARING OUR ESCAPE ACE IN THE HOLE. HOLD THAT POSE BENSON!
W-WHAT ARE YOU DOING...
FWASSSH!
RUN DUDES!

QUICK! EVERYONE INSIDE, JUST IN CASE IT CAN STILL SEE US FROM THERE!

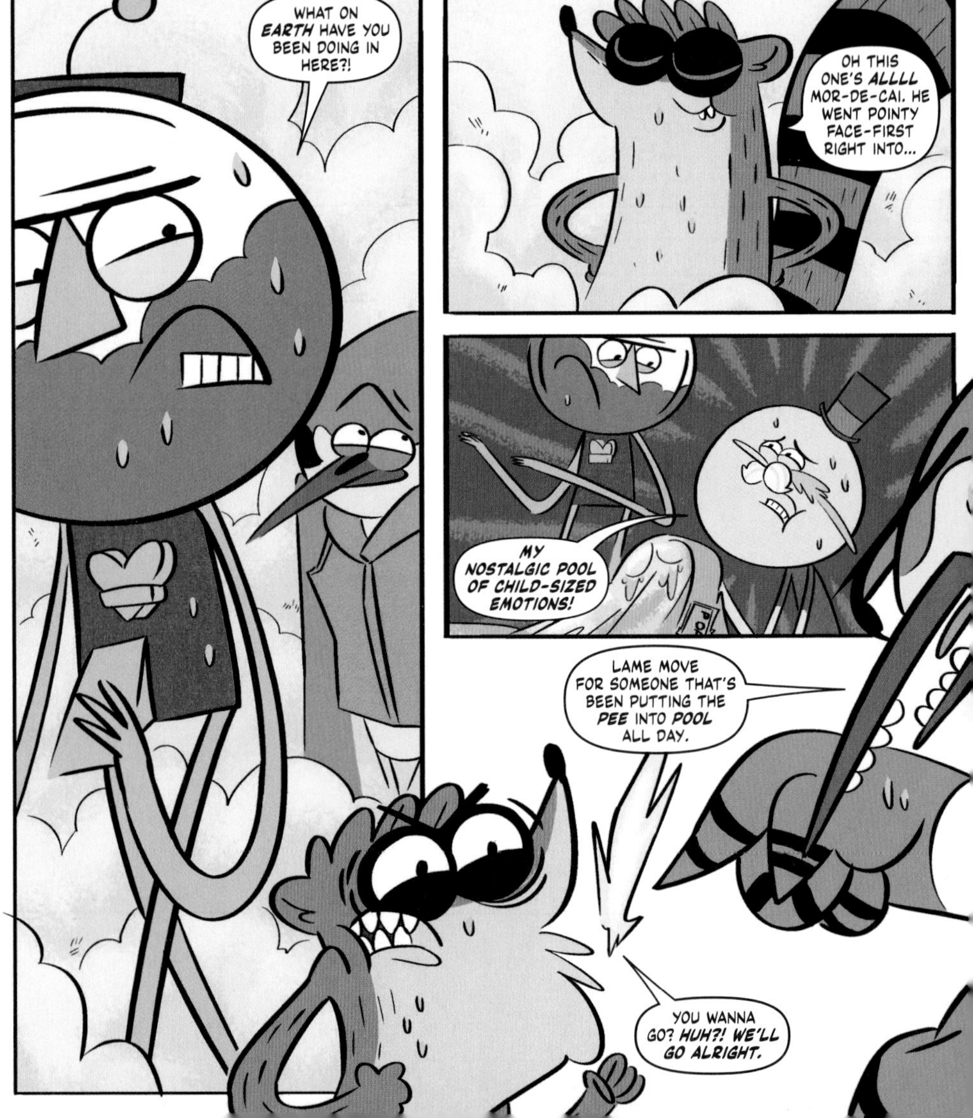
WHAT ON EARTH HAVE YOU BEEN DOING IN HERE?!
OH THIS ONE'S ALLLL MOR-DE-CAI. HE WENT POINTY FACE-FIRST RIGHT INTO...
MY NOSTALGIC POOL OF CHILD-SIZED EMOTIONS!
LAME MOVE FOR SOMEONE THAT'S BEEN PUTTING THE PEE INTO POOL ALL DAY.
YOU WANNA GO? HUH?! WE'LL GO ALRIGHT.

RRRRRRRRRRRRRRRRRRRRRRRRRRRR

COOL IT. WE'LL DEAL WITH BOTH YOUR FIREABLE OFFENSES LATER ON, BUT FIRST: ANY BRIGHT IDEAS ON SAVING THE PARK?

IT SEEMS LIKE THAT HYDRA DOESN'T REACT WELL TO TOTALLY GROSS THINGS, LIKE RIGBY...

OH WILL YOU LET IT GO ALREADY! MY "ACCIDENT" SAVED OUR HIDES!

...AS I WAS SAYING, THE ONLY GROSSER PERSON THAN RIGBY I CAN THINK OF RIGHT NOW IS PERFECT FOR WATER-SLIDE DEMOLITION!

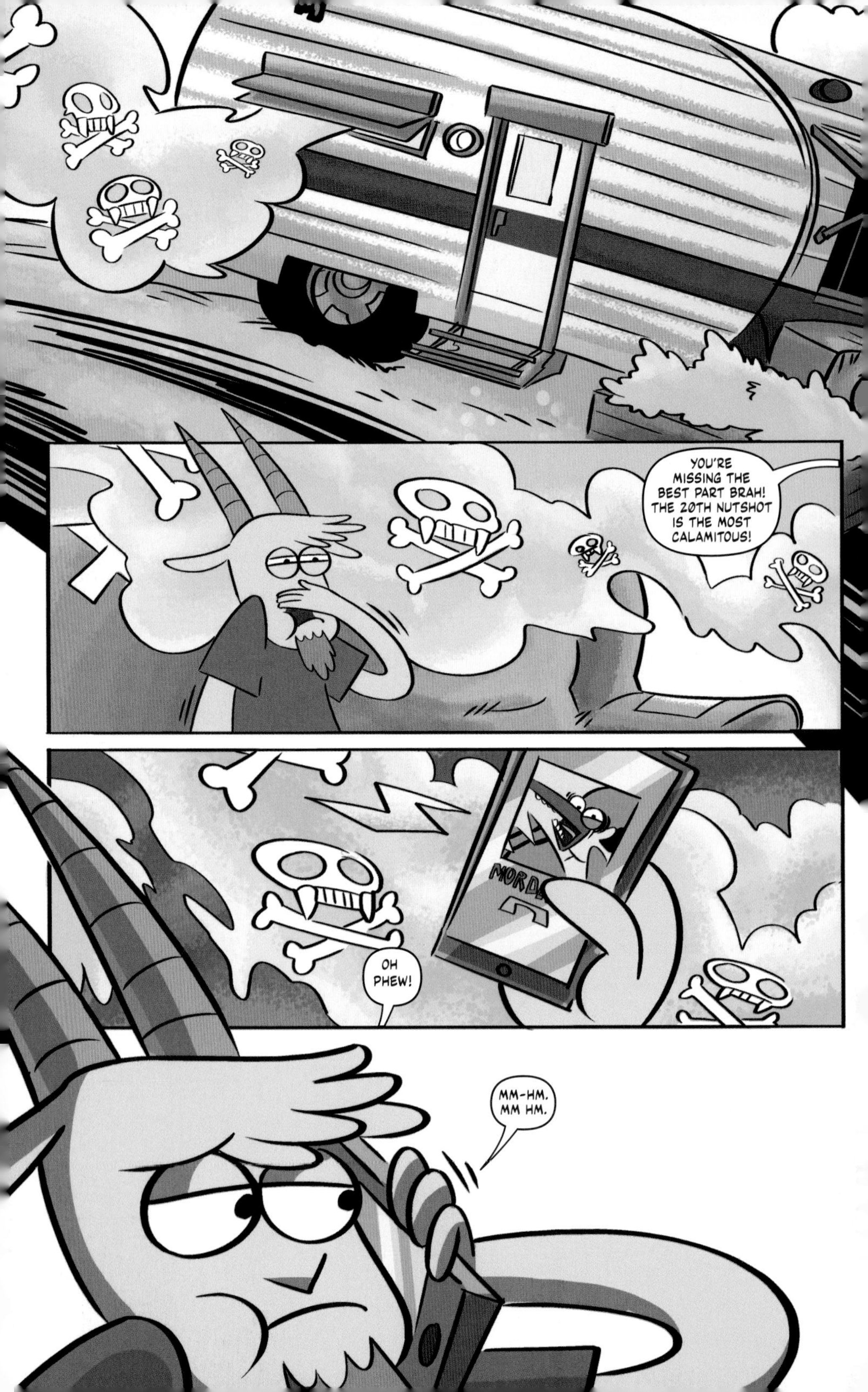
YOU'RE MISSING THE BEST PART BRAH! THE 20TH NUTSHOT IS THE MOST CALAMITOUS!
OH PHEW!
MM-HM. MM HM.

MUSC--ERK--LE MAN! MORDO JUST PHONED AND SAID A GREAT BIG MYTHICAL SNAKE BEAST WITH WATER SLIDES FOR NECKS HAS ATTACKED THE PARK AND IT HAS YOUR NAME ALLLL ⩥GACK⩤ OVER IT.
YOU KNOW WHAT ELSE HAS MY NAME ALLLL OVER IT?
NO. I HAVE ABSOLUTELY NO EARTHLY IDEA.
MY MOM!

I SHALL CHOOSE TO SPEND THE REST OF MY LIFE IN A SAUNA OF SUCH SERENITY!

HE'S ON HIS WAY. I'VE SEEN MUSCLE MAN WRECK MORE WATER SLIDES THAN PIZZA POUCHES HAVE FLAVORS. THIS ONE'S IN THE BAG!
IT BETTER BE!

LET'S STOP FIGHTING. NO MATTER HOW MANY GROSS THINGS I ***ACCIDENTALLY*** DO, I'LL NEVER TOP MUSCLE MAN'S INTENTIONAL GROSS-OCITY, AND WE'RE STILL FRIENDS WITH HIM, RIGHT?

I DUNNO DUDE...
DO SNAKES HAVE BUTTS? I WILL SOON ANSWER THIS MYSTERY!

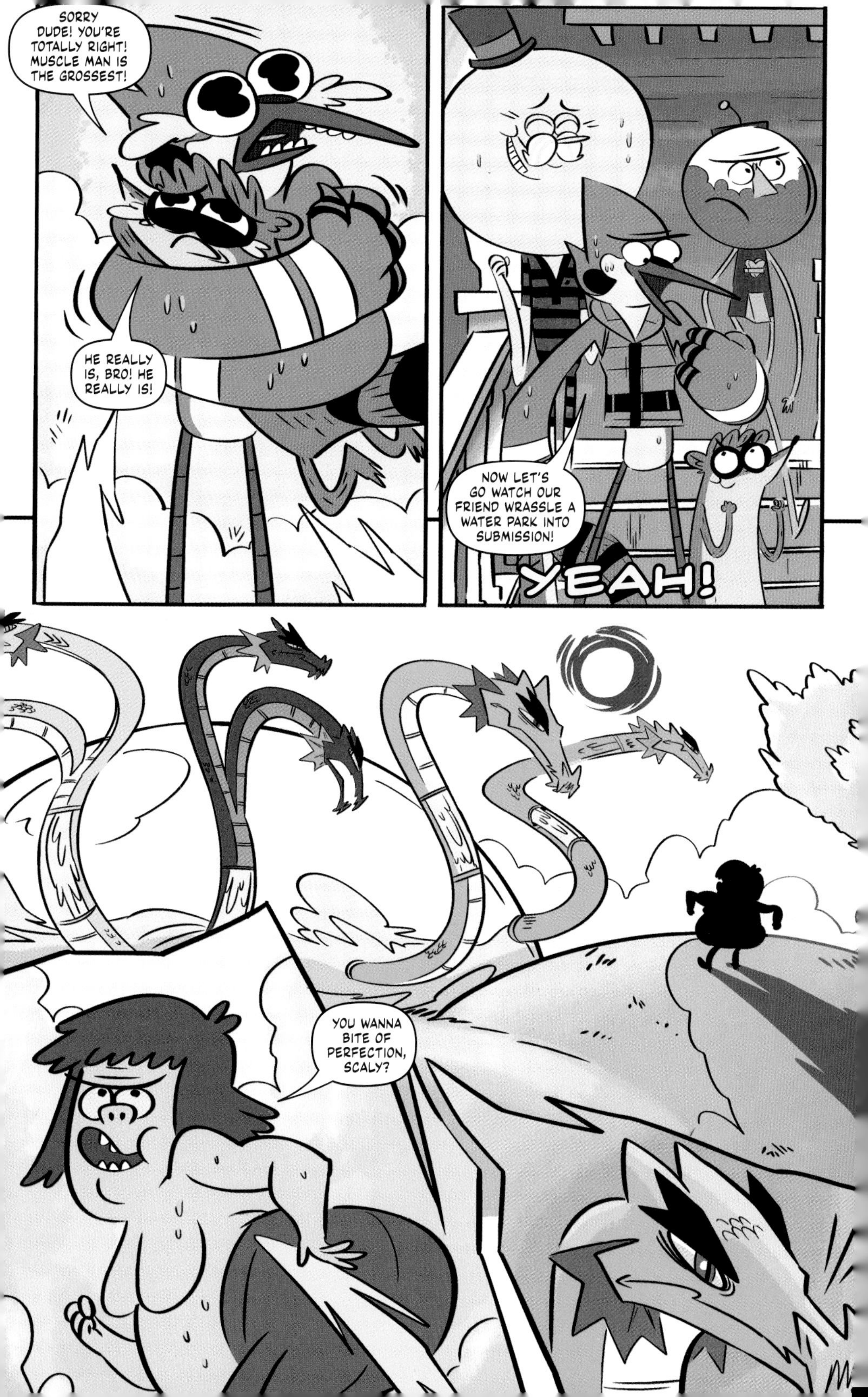
SORRY DUDE! YOU'RE TOTALLY RIGHT! MUSCLE MAN IS THE GROSSEST!
HE REALLY IS, BRO! HE REALLY IS!
NOW LET'S GO WATCH OUR FRIEND WRASSLE A WATER PARK INTO SUBMISSION!
YEAH!
YOU WANNA BITE OF PERFECTION, SCALY?

WATER PARK LOOKED ENTICING, STARTED SLITHERING AND SLICING, NOW IT'S LOOKING FRIGHTENED!
MUSCLE MAN K.OHHHHHHHH!
I WAS PROMISED A FEROCIOUS WATER SLIDE SERPENT BEAST! NOT A TOTALLY WUSSY WORM!
SSSSSSS!
WHY ISN'T THE SNAKE TRYING TO BITE MUSCLE MAN'S HOOHOO-DILLY'S OFF?
OH! MAYBE IT'S BECAUSE SNAKES SENSE MOST THINGS WITH SMELL...

...AND RIGHT NOW, MUSCLE MAN HAS AN UNAPPROACHABLE ODOR TO HIM!

WOO!
OHHHHHHHH!

HEY GUYS! MUSCLE MAN TOOK OFF ON HIS OWN AND...
YSS!
HSSSAAA!

NOOOOOOO!
OHHHH THAT CAN'T BE GOOD.
KAFF! KAFF! KAFF!

HEAVENS TO BETSY!
IT'S BREAKING FREE OF THE PARK!

...YET ANOTHER HUGE MYTHICAL BEAST ERUPTING FROM THE PARK, THE FIFTH THIS CALENDAR MONTH...

AAAAAAAAAH

GET IN! WE'VE GOT TO STOP IT SOMEHOW!

WHAT IF THAT WASN'T A SHOOTING STAR I WISHED ON FOR ULTIMATE COOLNESS LAST NIGHT...BUT THIS THING LANDING IN THE PARK!
YOU *WISHED* FOR THIS?!
NOT *THIS!* IF YOU HADN'T MADE ME SO SWEATY AND MISERABLE, I WOULDN'T HAVE WISHED FOR ANYTHING AND THE WORLD WOULDN'T BE ENDING!

NO TIME FOR THE BLAME GAME MORDECAI! LOOKS LIKE IT'S HEADING TO THE COFFEE SHOP TO PUT THE SQUEEZE...ON YOUR MAIN SQUEEZE!

OH NO... *MARGARET!*

INSIDE...
PIES
MUFFIN

...AND THEN ITS TAIL COMES DOWN LIKE *WHAM* AND SQUISHES THEM ALL!
OHHHH THAT SCENE'S TOTALLY DIFFERENT IN THE LIMITED EDITION LASER DISC REPRINT!

WHAT DID YOU SAY THAT GROUP OVER THERE WERE CALLED AGAIN?
OH! THE KAIJU CONNECT.

THEY MEET-UP EVERY WEEK TO TALK ABOUT GIANT MONSTER MOVIES AND THE ACTION FIGURES THEY COLLECT OF THEM.

HEY, KAIJOS. WHAT'RE YOUR FAVORITE MONSTER MOVIE MOMENTS THEN?
OH IT'S GOTTA BE THE STREET LEVEL CLOSE UP ON THE MONSTER'S EYES! SUCH DEPTH. MUCH BEAUTY.

WOW. LIKE THAT?
SSSSSSSS!

C'MON, C'MON, PICK UP, *PICK UP* YOU...

BABY DUCKS
calling
YO MORDECAI!
BABY DUCKS!

YOU GOTTA COME QUICK! THERE'S THIS GIANT HYDRA WATER PARK THING WRECKING THE CITY AND AND AND...

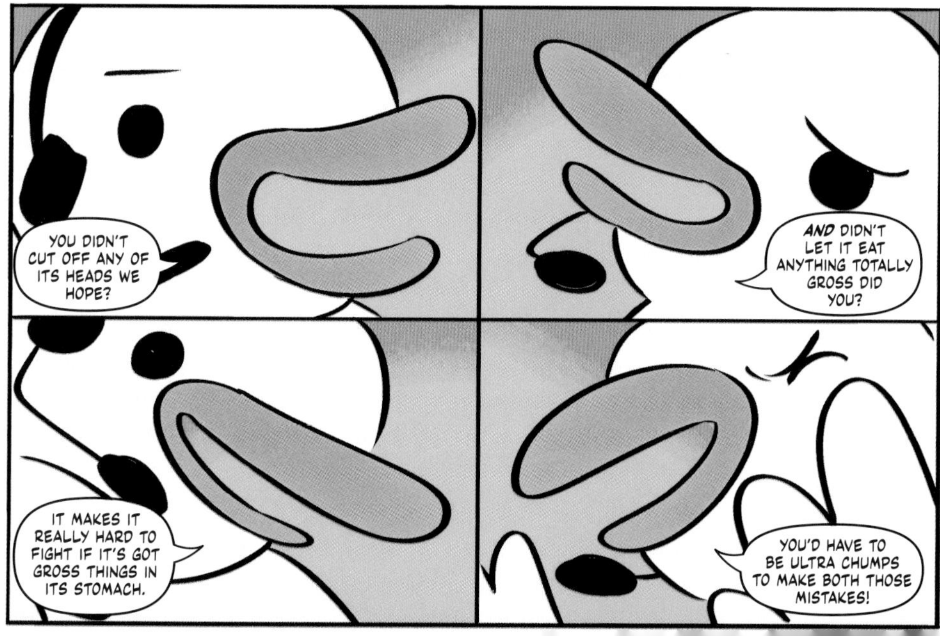
YOU DIDN'T CUT OFF ANY OF ITS HEADS WE HOPE?
AND DIDN'T LET IT EAT ANYTHING TOTALLY GROSS DID YOU?
IT MAKES IT REALLY HARD TO FIGHT IF IT'S GOT GROSS THINGS IN ITS STOMACH.
YOU'D HAVE TO BE ULTRA CHUMPS TO MAKE BOTH THOSE MISTAKES!

UHHHHH...
PLEASE HURRY!
ALREADY HERE! WE SAW IT ON THE NEWS...
...AND KNEW YOU LOSERS WOULD NEED OUR HELP RIGHT AWAY!

THINK YOU CAN TAKE HIM?
I DUNNO... IT LOOKS LIKE IT HAS POISON LUH-LUH-LUH LASERS!
HOW'D IT GET THEM, THOUGH...
LET'S DO THE FUSION THING AGAIN AND WHOOP ITS SNAKY BUTT IN DOUBLE TIME! ESPECIALLY SINCE WE HAVE POPS AND BENSON TO HELP TOO!
I ADORE FUCHSIAS!
UHHH...
FIST PUMP LIKE YOUR LIVES SORT-OF DEPEND ON IT!

ICE PIZZA
I'M EGGSELLENT
HSS?
FWASH!

YEAH! NOW WE'RE SUPER EAGLE-MAN TURBO EDITION!
I'M EGGSELLENT

WHY AM I IN THIS THING? WHY DON'T I GET ANY CONTROLS?
I'M EGGSELLENT
YOU'RE HOOKED IN DIRECTLY TO OUR RAGE METER, BENSON. THE ANGRIER YOU GET, THE MORE POWERFUL WE BECOME.
I'M EGGSELLENT
OH BENSOOOON... I TOTALLY SMASHED UP THE FRIDGE-FREEZER BIG-TIME TODAY!
RRRRRIGBY!
RRRRRRRR

ROUND ONE!
I'M EGGSELLENT
ROCKET PUNCH!
WHAMMY!
FAPPO!

FSHOOOOO!
FACE FULL OF STINK WATER? I DON'T THINK SO! PUMP IT UP!
I'M EGGSELLENT
SONIC SHIELD!

I'M EGGSELLENT
'M ELLENT
PLAY US A TUNE, POPS!
OH JOLLY GOOD SHOW!

BRO, WE'RE WINNING! THIS IS A CINCH!
I'M EGGSELLENT
I KNOW! WE'RE TOTALLY CLEANING ITS CLOCK! EASIEST FINAL BOSS EVAH!
I'M EGGSELLENT
CRACKKK!
I'M EGGSELLENT
WILL YOU IDIOTS KEEP YOUR EYES ON THE PRIZE!

OH A MECHA VERSUS MANY-HEADED ADVERSARY! I LOVE THIS DYNAMIC.
DID YOU ATTEND ONE OF THESE?
NOT SAYING.
I'LL BET MY MR. MOTHAGON PLAY SET ON A TOTAL K.O. VICTORY!
I RAISE YOU MY TORTOI-TRON IX TRANSMOGRIFIER THAT IT DEVOURS THEM IN ONE GULP!
TORTOI-TRON IX TRANSMOGRIFIER
MR MOTHAGON
THOSE ARE OUR FRIENDS FIGHTING OUT THERE! IF THEY LOSE, IT'LL EAT US ALL!
WOULD YOU CARE TO WAGER WHICH OF US IT EATS FIRST?

WOW, THE PARK LOOKS PRETTY TOTALLED FROM UP HERE.
GRAAAAHHHH!
I'M
SHOOOMMM

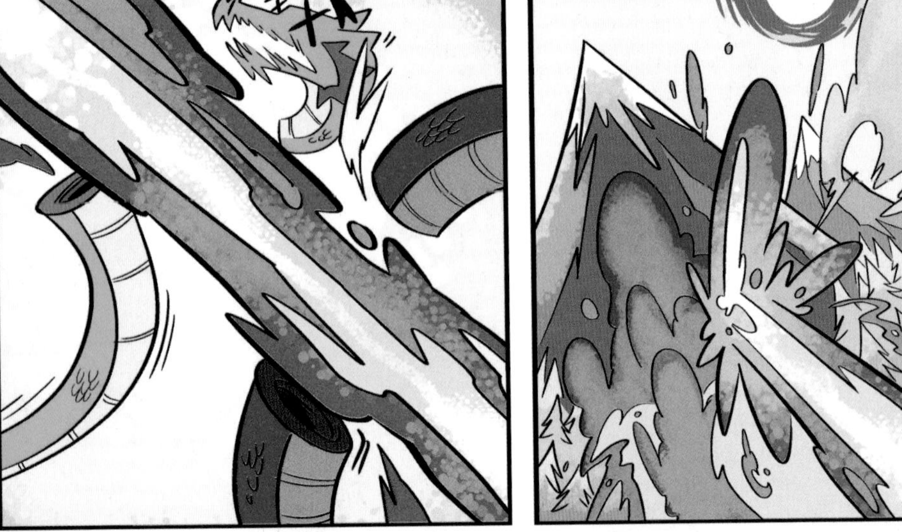

I'M EGGSELLENT
THAT WAS SUPER-SWEET BUT...
I'M EGGSELLENT
WE PROBABLY SHOULDN'T SHOOT THAT ONE OFF AGAIN!

I'M EGGSELLENT

I'M EGGSELLENT
OH, LOOKS LIKE WE CAN'T ANYWAY. EHEHEHE. BENSON'S NAPPING ON THE JOB...
OH NAP-TIME SOUNDS DELIGHTFUL!
NO POPS! NO NAP-TIME!

I'M EGGSELLE
DUDES! SOME HELP HERE?

CLOSSSSE BUT NO CCCCIGAARRRR!

YOU CAN SPEAK?!
IF A GIANT CHICKEN CAN SSSSPEAK, WHY SSSSHOULDN'T WE?
I'M EGGSELLENT
HE HAS A POINT I GUESS.
IT SAID WE WERE 'CLOSE', MAYBE IF WE GOT ALL ITS HEADS IN ONE GO...
GREAT MINDS, MORDECAI!

PUMPFFFF
LET'S SEE IF SNAKE BUTT LIKES EATING POWER SWORD, YOOOooO--!

I'M EGGSELLENT
I'M EGGSELLENT
'M EGGSELLENT
SLICE!

I'M
EGGSELLEN

BEATING LOSER SNAKES FEELS LIKE SECOND NATURE! ANY GIANT DEMON-DOGS TO TAKE CARE OF TOO, BROS?
PSSSSSSSS!
PSSSSSSSSSSSSYCHE!

I'M EGGSELLENT
I'M EGGSELLENT
I'M EGGSELLENT
OH IT'S SNEAKY TALKING SNAKES I DETEST THE MOST!
NOW ITSSSS OUR TURN TO GIVE YOU A SSSSSSSSLAP!
I'M EGGSELLENT

SSSSSSSSUPER NO MORE, YOU SSSSSSSSILLY DUCKSSSSSSSSS!
SSSSSSSSORT YOUR LISP OUT BRO!
STOP
QUICK, EVERYBODY INTO THIS SKETCHY ALLEY-WAY!

WE'RE DOOMED! IF SUPER EAGLE-MAN TURBO EDITION COULDN'T GET THE JOB DONE, WE'LL NEED SOME MIRACLE MAKING SUPER-WIZARD TO MAGIC IT AWAY!
WOULD YOU SETTLE FOR... THE WIZARD OF LIZARDS!?
COME AGAIN?

STARE
STARE

COUGH
AWWWKWARD
COUGH

WE WANNA TALK TO THIS WEIRD LIZARD GUY REAL QUICK. YOU GONNA BE OKAY FIGHTING ALONE FOR NOW, BRO?
YOU GUYS WERE CRAMPING OUR STYLE ANYWAY! WE'VE EATEN BIGGER WORMS FOR BREAKFAST!
WHILE WE'VE EATEN BIGGER CHICKEN WINGSSSS FOR SSSSNACKSSSS!

KRACK
SALUTATIONS. I AM HERE TO HELP RELIEVE YOU OF YOUR REPTILE PROBLEM. IF YOU'D CARE TO JOIN ME...
...IN MY BASE OF OPERATIONS.
LIZRO
EEEEEEEHHHHH...

THANK YOU. MY OTHER NAME IS WILLIAM SARDINGTON AND I AM BUT A HUMBLE HERPETOLOGIST ON THE ROAD TRYING TO RIGHT A GRIEVOUS WRONG...
YOU'RE A 'TOLOGIST OF WHAT AGAIN, WILLY?
A HERPETOLOGIST?
RIGBY!
AAAA-HA -HA-HA!
OH. VERY GOOD, TOP SHELF. IT MEANS I AM AN EXPERT IN REPTILES AND AMPHIBIANS.

BEFORE WE START, ANYONE FOR TEA? PERFECT ANTIDOTE FOR SUCH A SWELTERING DAY!
I'LL HAVE A CUP, FINE SIR!
RRRRRRRR!
NOTHING QUITE LIKE A REFRESHING HOT CUP OF TEA ON A SUMMER'S DAY...

HOLD UP, NO WAY, THAT'S JUST MORE HOT JUICE!

DON'T TRY TO CLOAK BOILING LIES WITH A FANCY NEW LABEL.

HOT JUICE UNTRUTHS HAVE ALREADY COST ME MUCH THIS DAY...!
RAAAAH!
NOOOOOOOO!
KER-SAVE!
NO! NO. YOU MUST ALWAYS DRINK TEA RESPONSIBLY.

WHAT IS *WRONG* WITH YOU RIGBY?! THIS TWEE BRITISH MAN IS TRYING TO HELP US...
BRITISH?! OH HOW SIMPLY SPLENDID. ALLOW ME TO GREET YOU IN THE APPROPRIATE MANNER...
NO PINKY FINGER?! THIS GENT HAS NO PINKY FINGER FOR THE SPECIAL HANDSHAKE?

AH, ABOUT THAT. IT ALL STARTED...
WOAH WOAH WOAH. HOLD IT THERE. MY GIANT FLASHBACK SENSE IS TINGLING BUT...
MEANWHILE...
KAAPOOOW
UGHHH.
CLEANERS
NO PARKING
2.99
USA
OPEN

SSS HSSS HSSS HSS! WEAKSSSSSSSSSAUCE.

STEP OFF!

HSS!
HSS!
HSS!

NOT COOL.

THEY'LL BE FINE! THOSE BABY DUCKS CAN TAKE CARE OF...
NO PARKI
USA TONITE
SHOOOM!
DUDE! ARE YOU OKAY?!
NOT DOIN' SO HOT, BRO...
MORDECAI!

COFFEE SHOP
AAH! M-MARGARET! AND EILEEN.

2.99
IS THERE ANYTHING WE CAN DO TO HELP?
YEAH, SERIOUSLY. CAN'T BELIEVE THOSE LOSERS INSIDE ARE STILL BETTING AGAINST THE GOOD GUYS...

WE'RE ABOUT TO FIND OUT FROM AN EXPERT GUY HOW TO FINISH THIS THING OFF AND THE BABY DUCKS WERE GOING TO DISTRACT THAT HYDRA THING WHILE WE DO BUT...UNLESS YOU'RE LIKE REALLY ***REALLY*** GOOD AT FIST-PUMPING I DUNNO WHAT...
FIST PUMP ARE ONE OF MY FAVORITE BANDS! OF COURSE I CAN FIST PUMP WITH THE BEST OF THEM.

I HAVE ALSO BEEN KNOWN TO OFFER UP A FINE FIST PUMP OR TWO ON OCCASION.
WELL ONLY IF THE BABY DUCKS ARE...
WE'RE COOL WITH IT. TOTALLY.
2.99
STOP

COFFEE SHOP
MORDECAI $ THE RIGBY'S
I HOPE THIS WASN'T A MISTAKE...

MORDECAI & THE RIGBY'S
MORDECAI & THE RIGBY'S
WOAH! AWESOME!
SUPREME.

LET'S DO THIS, EILEEN!
...MY ALLERGIES...
ALREADY?!
MORDECAI & RIGBY'S
EMERGENCY

HSSSSSSSST!!

SPLUSHOOOM!

YOU ONLY HAVE TO KEEP IT AT BAY FOR A BIT! GOOD LUCK!
GROAN
MORDECAI & THE RIGBY'S
MORDECAI & THE RIGBY'S
YOU HEARD HIM! LET'S PUT THIS CREEP IN ITS PLACE!
FORE!
KWANG!

BRAKA-BOOM!
OKAY! FLASHBACK TIME: GOOOOOOOO!
BORN INTO THE SARDINGTON ESTATE, MY TALE TRULY BEGINS DURING MY UNIVERSITY YEARS, WHERE I STUDIED BIOLOGY AND MADE WILD NEW FRIENDS AND TEA-ENTHUSIASTS...

DORM
PERHAPS TOO WILD AS I WOULD LEARN ON MY TWENTY-FIRST BIRTHDAY...

WE WERE ALWAYS LOOKING TO RE-INVIGORATE THE RUSH OF DRINKING A FINE CUP OF TEA IN NEW AND INTERESTING PLACES.
BLOODY HOOLIGANS!

WATER WORLD
"WHICH LEAD US TO A WATER PARK IN THE DEAD OF NIGHT THAT WE SCANDALOUSLY SNEAKED INTO WITHOUT PERMISSION.
NO
"THE CHALLENGE DE JOUR WAS TO RIDE THE SLIDES WITHOUT SPILLING A DROP OF PRECIOUS TEA."
WATER WORLD
OH THAT SOUNDS LIKE AN ABSOLUTE RIOT FOR SUCH BRITISH RASCALS!

"FOR ENGLAND, WILLIAM.
WATERWORLD
"MY COMPATRIOT ACHIEVED THE GOAL WITH LITTLE TO NO DIFFICULTY.
"I FELT ON TOP OF THE WORLD AT THAT TIME IN PARTICULAR.
"I'D NEVER FELT SO ALIVE. THE REFRESHING COOL WATER SLIDING AGAINST ME, THE CAPTIVATING AROMA OF A FRESH BREW..."

BUMP!
SPILL!
"THAT ALL CHANGED IN AN INSTANT.
KER-SLICE!
"THEY WOULDN'T TELL ME STRAIGHT AT FIRST..."

"...BUT I WOULD NEVER BE ABLE TO DRINK TEA IN THE MANNER OF A DISTINGUISHED GENTLEMAN EVER AGAIN.

"WITHOUT THE DALLIANCE OF TEA-DRINKING, I GRADUATED WITH HONORS IN BIOLOGY...

"...AND SET OUT ON MY LIFE'S WORK AS A HERPETOLOGIST...

"...AND THE STUDY OF REPTILES' REGENERATIVE PROPERTIES!"

AH AH! YOU SHOULDA READ MORE COMICS INSTEAD OF GETTING A DUMB DIPLOMA. LIZARD WHACKO SCIENCE NEVER WORKS OUT WELL!
"I WASN'T JUST DABBLING IN 'LIZARD WHACKO SCIENCE' HOWEVER...
IV
V
III
"...I WAS ALSO CONSUMED BY THE THOUGHT OF DESIGNING THE SAFEST WATER-PARK EVER CONCEIVED...

"..WHERE ONE COULD SIMULTANEOUSLY SIP TEA AS WELL AS SLIDE.

"I WOULD ENCASE THEM IN GLASS DOMES TO ENSURE NOTHING COULD INTERFERE WITH THE AERODYNAMIC TESTING PROCESS OF THE SLIDES."

"MY TWO OBSESSIONS REQUIRED FAR MORE SPACE THAN MY MODEST LODGINGS COULD ACCOMMODATE HOWEVER...
YOU SHOULD TRY SHARING A ROOM WITH RIGBY. SOMETIMES I CAN'T BUDGE AN INCH FROM RANDOM TRASH PILED IN.
SODA
THANK YOU
"...AHEM, WELL, I HAD TO SEEK OUT A SEPARATE SPACE FOR MY EXPERIMENTAL ENDEAVOURS...
"...TIME WAS OF THE ESSENCE."

"EAGER TO GET STARTED WITH MY LIFE'S WORK IN EARNEST, I TOOK THE FIRST PLACE I COULD FIND.
STORAGE
"I WAS EXCITED TO GET TO WORK, ESPECIALLY SINCE I HAD COME INTO POSSESSION OF A RARE MUTANT PYTHON...
"...WHO REALLY DIDN'T SEEM TO LIKE ME VERY MUCH.
"I'LL NEVER KNOW WHY."
BOOKS
SODA

"I WOULD SOON FIND OUT I SHARED THE BUILDING WITH AN ECLECTIC MIX OF ECCENTRIC INDIVIDUALS."
AH AH. AS A LANDLORD MYSELF TOO MANY ODD TENANTS IN CLOSE PROXIMITY IS A RECIPE FOR DISASTER.

"A RECIPE FOR DISASTER INDEED."

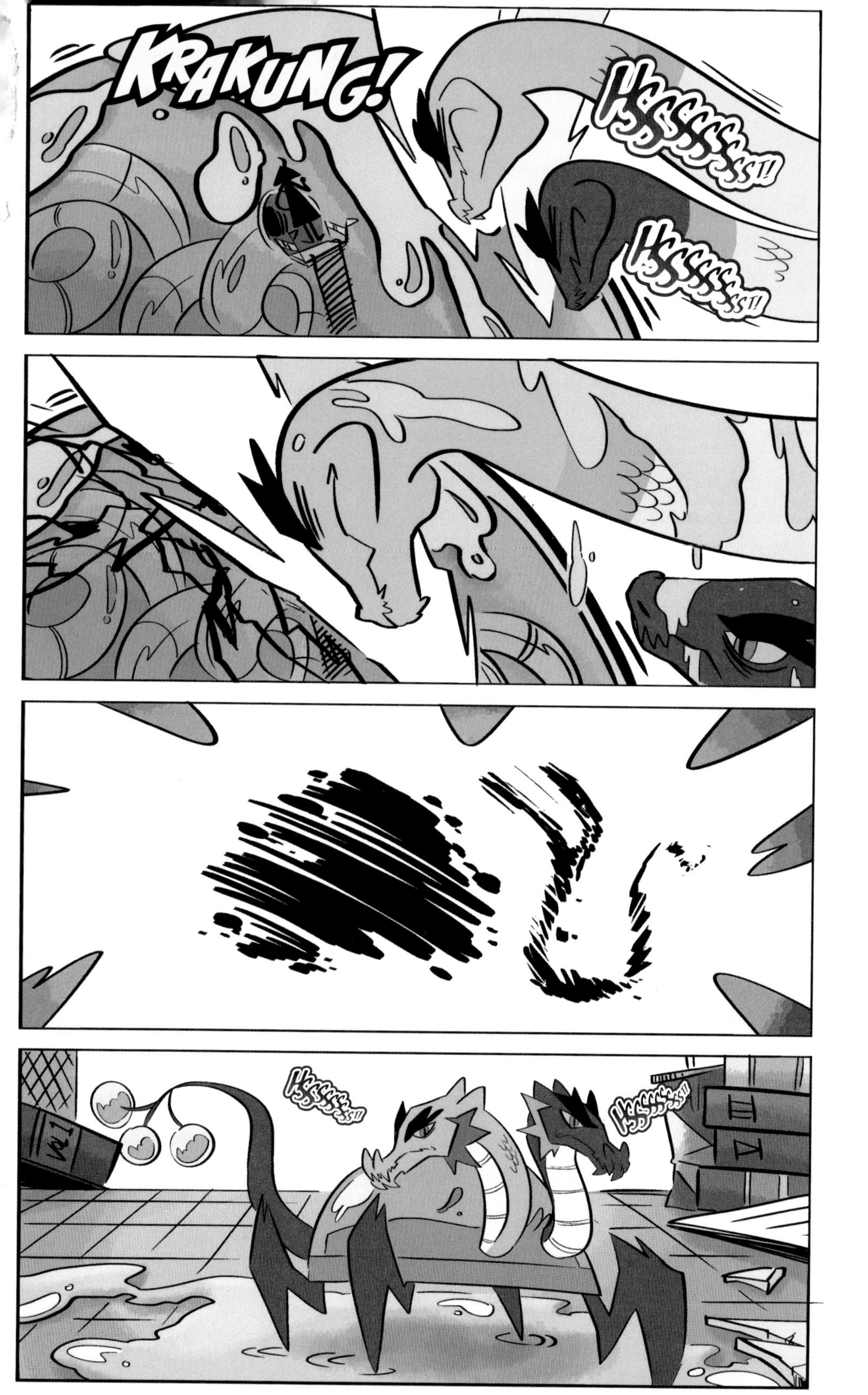
KRAKUNG!
HSSSSSSSST!!
HSSSSSSSST!!
HSSSSSSSST!!
Vol. 1
HSSSSSSSST!!

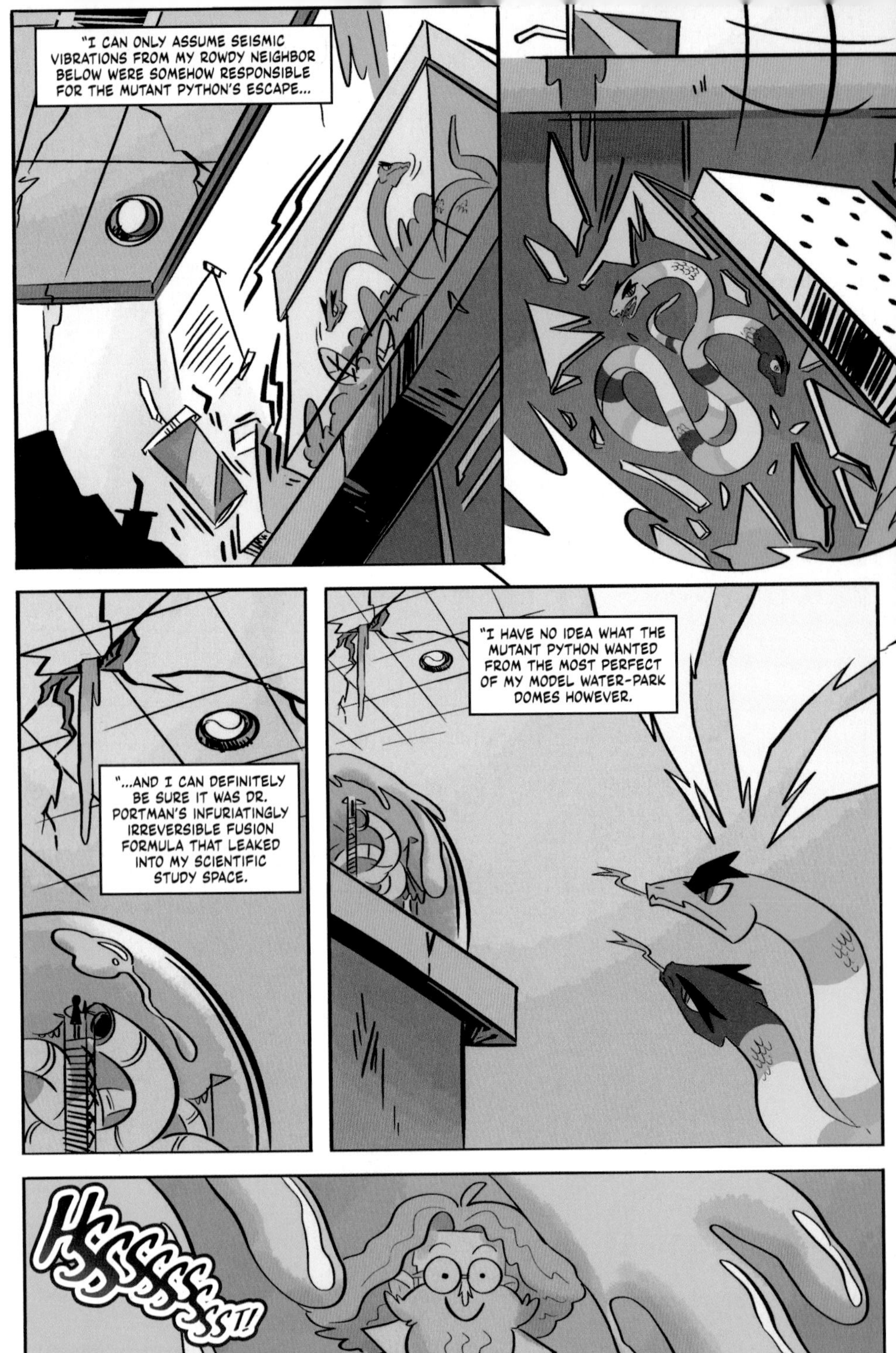
"I CAN ONLY ASSUME SEISMIC VIBRATIONS FROM MY ROWDY NEIGHBOR BELOW WERE SOMEHOW RESPONSIBLE FOR THE MUTANT PYTHON'S ESCAPE...
"...AND I CAN DEFINITELY BE SURE IT WAS DR. PORTMAN'S INFURIATINGLY IRREVERSIBLE FUSION FORMULA THAT LEAKED INTO MY SCIENTIFIC STUDY SPACE.
"I HAVE NO IDEA WHAT THE MUTANT PYTHON WANTED FROM THE MOST PERFECT OF MY MODEL WATER-PARK DOMES HOWEVER.

"NO IDEA AT ALL."

"I CAN ONLY ASSUME THE RESULTING BEAST DOWNED EVERY LAST DROP OF MY MOST POTENT REGROWTH HORMONE FORMULA.

"IT'S PREPOSTEROUS TO ME THAT I WAS EVICTED, CONSIDERING I WAS CONDUCTING THE MOST SAFE SCIENCE IN THE WHOLE ACCURSED COMPLEX.

"I WOULD SOON HAVE TO LEAVE MY OLD LIFE ENTIRELY HOWEVER...
YOUR AD

"...AND GIVE CHASE TO THIS CONNIVING BEAST ALL ACROSS THE WORLD."
NO PAR

WELL NOW WE KNOW WHEN TO CELEBRATE THIS NIGHTMARE'S BIRTHDAY BUT THERE'S STILL NO WAY TO SPLODE IT!

ANY IDEA WHAT GETS IT ALL RILED UP? IT SEEMED TO HATE RIGBY AND MUSCLE MAN IN PARTICULAR...

head
core
APOLOGIES. WHAT IS CLEAR TO ME IS YOU MUST DESTROY THE CORE THAT HAS FUSED WITH THE GLASS DOME AND WATER PARK MODEL.

IT SEEMS TO HATE POOR HYGIENE MORE THAN ANYTHING ELSE. NO IDEA WHY. NONE. NO IDEA AT ALL.

PERSECUTION! IT'S A PERSECUTION PARTY!

I HAVE HAD SUCH A TRAUMATIC DAY! LAVA-DEATH BY ASSOCIATION, BRAIN FREEZE HALLUCINATIONS, AND AN INTAKE OF SO MUCH HOT-JUICE I WAS READY TO...
EXPLODE!
WHY THANK YOU MORDECAI, I...
WE JUST NEED TO MAKE THE HYDRA EXPLODE FROM THE INSIDE FROM GETTING IT TO EAT ITS OWN HEADS!
AHA YES! EVERY TIME A HYDRA HEAD DEGENERATES IT BECOMES LIKE WATER, AND THE REGENERATION PROCESS ALSO PRODUCES VAST AMOUNTS OF AQUA PURA IN TURN! ENOUGH VOLUME AND...
...EXPLODEY!

WHILE I'M SURE THE HYDRA WON'T HESITATE TO CHASE ME DOWN ITS OWN THROAT IN RAGE DUE TO WHATEVER GRUDGE IT BEARS, HOW WILL ALL YOU FELLOWS ENRAGE IT?
TRASH ONLY!
WELL SINCE YOU ALL THINK I HAVE AN APTITUDE FOR GROSS-OCITY, MAY I SUGGEST A HUMBLE DUMPSTER DIVE OR TWO?
ERRRRR...

C'MON, YOU SQUARES. LETS. GET. STINKY!

MORDECAI & THE RIGBY'S
THERMAL SCOPE ACTIVATED.
SCANNING
COUNTING TOTAL: 112_
TOXIC LEVEL 96%
HIGH
SURVIVOR
HI-5s
GROSS
SKIPS
THERE'S OVER A HUNDRED PEOPLE IN THAT THING'S BELLY! OTHER THAN MUSCLE-MAN THEY ALL LOOK LIKE THEY'RE NOT HOLDING UP TOO WELL...
MORDECAI & THE RIGBY'S

STOP
THANKS GIRLS! CATCH YA LATER!
FIRST WE'LL DRAW IT BACK TO THE PARK, AWAY FROM THE CITY AND THEN SPLIT INTO THE AGREED TEAMS.
PARK→
YO! STINKY TOO-MANY-SNAKE-FACES! DO ONE!
HSSSSSSS!!
SSSSARDINGTON!
PARK
GET SOME DISTANCE AND THEN LET'S GET READY FOR OPERATION: ALL YOU CAN EAT SNAKE-HEAD BUFFET!

ME NEITHER. MY ALLERGIES ARE GETTING ALLERGIES, MARGARET. I DON'T THINK I CAN LAST MUCH LONGER...
MORDECAI & THE RIGBY'S
I REALLY DON'T WANT TO TURN MY OWN CAR INTO A JUNK MISSILE EITHER...
LICENS
STOP! WE'VE GOT THE PLAN NOW! WE NEED THE BABY DUCKS HELP THOUGH. YOU CAN...ER... UN-TRANSFORM NOW?
WOAH!
WOAH!

MEANWHILE...
HOLD ON, KIDS!
THANKS, MR. SKIPS! I COULDN'T STAND THAT GUYS B.O. FOR MUCH LONGER...
ME NEITHER. THOUGHT I'D GET YOU KIDS OUT FIRST THEN GO BACK FOR MORE OF THE ADULTS...
DAYLIGHT!

READY!

I WILL HAVE MY VENGEANC-CCCCCCCCCCCCE!

POSITIONS, PEOPLE!

YOU COST ME MY LABORATORY, YOU REPTILE DELINQUENT!
YOU SSSSLOVENLY DISSSSGRACE! I'LL CONSSSSUME YOU WHOLE!
BY ALL MEANS!
FINALLY! THE PERFECTLY DESIGNED TEA-DRINKING WATERSLIDE EXPERIENCE!

THANKS FOR RUINING MY PARK YOU JERK! A MIRACLE TURNED MENACE!

HSSSSSSSST!
HSSSSSSSST!
OH DRIVING SLIDE-WAYS IS MY FAVOURITE!
WEE HEE HEE! A REFRESHING AFTERNOON'S DRIVE TO WASH AWAY THE SMELLIES!

WOAH, DUDE!
GUFFF!
BOWURRP!
THE POOL DESSSSSSSSSECRATOR! THE ABSSSSOLUTE WORSSSSSSSST ONE YET!
ACTUALLY, I'M...
...THE BESSSST ONE EVER!

ERRR... HERE SNAKEY SNAKEY?
DUDE, LAME!
SNORT
TAP TAP
COME ON MAN. GET CHASIN' ME!
YOU DON'T SSSSMELL LIKE THE OTHERS. YOU'RE BETTER THAN THISSSS.
UGH. I DIDN'T COVER MYSELF IN ENOUGH TRASH BECAUSE I WAS WORRIED MARGARET WOULD SMELL ME. WHAT DO I DO?!

NO! NOT WHAT WOULD I DO...WHAT WOULD RIGBY DO!
SKRITCH SKRITTTTCCH
BUUUUORRRPPPPO!
BUUOOFFF!
POOT! TOOT!

SSSSSSSSO BE IT!

FREE AT LAST!
QUICK! BACK DOWN THE CHUTE SKIPS!
WHA-?

MORDO-BOMB OF CERTAIN DOOM!

T-THIS IS THE END OF THE ⸗GACK⸗ ROAD FOR ME...
BROS!
TOTALLY ⸗HACK⸗ THE GROSSEST.
LUH-LUH-LUH LASERS!
NOW BABY DUDERS!

MORE LASERS FOR YOU, LOSER!
EVERYONE IN HERE! START FIST PUMPING LIKE YOUR LIFE DEPENDS ON IT!

STEP OFF!
KER-SPLODE!

POOF!

LASERS FOR BREAKFAST, LASERS FOR LUNCH, SNAKEY COULDN'T HANDLE DINNER, OR A SUPER EAGLE GUTPUNCH! OOOOOOOOH!

MAAAARCO!
...POLO...

MY WATER-PARK DESIGNS WERE BANG ON! NOT A DIGIT LOST!
HSSSSSSST!

THE PARK'S RUINED!
I HATE WATER PARKS.
LOOK ON THE BRIGHT SIDE, AT LEAST MUSCLE MAN FINALLY HAD A BATH!

THANKS RIGBY. MEMORIES OF YOU AND THINGS ONLY YOU CAN DO SAVED US ALL IN THE END!
AWWW THANKS MORDO. ALL THIS GRODY LIZARD GOO IS CHILLING ME TO THE BONE THOUGH DUDE...

BRRRR. ME TOO. I'VE GOT JUST THE THING FOR THE CHILLS THOUGH, BRO!

SCORE 1125
YAYEAAAAHHHH! WARMING GLOW OF DAT LAVA LEVEL!

PEAK ACHIEVED

THE END

SPRING 2015

REGULAR SHOW™

VOLUME 2

WRITTEN BY
RACHEL CONNOR

ILLUSTRATED BY
WOOK JIN CLARK